Put Beginning Readers on the Right Track with ALL ABOARD READING™

The All Aboard Reading series is especially for beginning readers. Written by noted authors and illustrated in full color, these are books that children really and truly *want* to read—books to excite their imagination, tickle their funny bone, expand their interests, and support their feelings. With three different reading levels, All Aboard Reading lets you choose which books are most appropriate for your children and their growing abilities.

Level 1—for Preschool through First Grade Children
Level 1 books have very few lines per page, very large type, easy words, lots of repetition, and pictures with visual "cues" to help children figure out the words on the page.

Level 2—for First Grade to Third Grade Children
Level 2 books are printed in slightly smaller type than Level 1 books. The stories are more complex but there is still lots of repetition in the text and many pictures. The sentences are quite simple and are broken up into short lines to make reading easier.

Level 3—for Second through Third Grade Children
Level 3 books have considerably longer texts, use harder words and more complicated sentences.

All Aboard for happy reading!

For my sister Diane,
may you never go without
a real birthday cake again!

Happy 7th birthday,
Janine!
Love,
Mom.

Library of Congress Cataloging-in-Publication Data
Cocca-Leffler, Maryann, 1958–   Ice-cold birthday / by Maryann Cocca-Leffler.   p.   cm.— (All aboard reading) Summary: A big snowstorm threatens to spoil a birthday party but also creates some unforeseen opportunities for special fun. [1. Birthdays—Fiction.   2. Snow—Fiction. 3. Blizzards—Fiction.]   I. Title.   II. Series. PZ7.C638Ic 1992 [E]—dc20
91-30456   CIP   AC

ISBN 0-448-40381-1 (GB)   A B C D E F G H I J
ISBN 0-448-40380-3 (pbk.)   A B C D E F G H I J

ALL
ABOARD
READING™

Level 1
Preschool–Grade 1

ICE-COLD BIRTHDAY

By Maryann Cocca-Leffler

Grosset & Dunlap • New York

Some people have all the luck!

I have luck too.

Bad luck.

The week before the dance show,

I broke my arm.

The year I held the flag
in the parade,
it rained.

And the day
of our class pictures,
I spilled green paint
all over my new dress.

But on my birthday
I was sure my luck would change.

My birthday started out great.

It was snowing!

Everything looked so pretty.

Dad made a birthday pancake.

It was a seven.

At school I got an A
in math.
But the best part
was still to come.
Six friends were
coming to my party.

After school I ran home.
The snow was
coming down hard.
And it was very windy.

Mom was
baking
a big cake.
Dad was
blowing up
balloons.

12

My sister set the table
with party plates and candy.
What a great party
this was going to be.

Then I heard the radio...

~BAD STORM IS HERE~
~TWO FEET OF SNOW~
~HIGH WINDS~

"Oh no! My party!" I said.

"Don't worry," said Dad.

"With luck
the storm will pass."

Luck? I have no luck!

That's when it happened.

The radio stopped playing.

The cake stopped baking.

All the lights went off.

The power was out.

Then the calls came.

No one could come

to my party.

"I knew it!
I knew it!"
I cried.

I put on my coat.

I sat down

and stared

at the blank TV.

No cake.

No party.

No fun.

Just an ice-cold

birthday!

Then Mom came in.

She had a funny cake.

It was made of ice cream
and cookies.

I had to smile.

I made a wish and blew out
the candles.

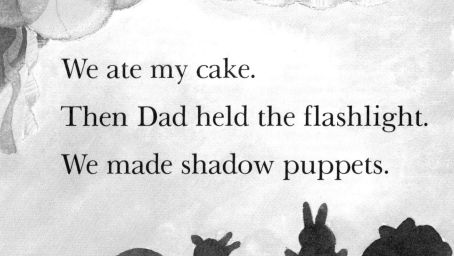

We ate my cake.

Then Dad held the flashlight.

We made shadow puppets.

Later, everybody played
pin-the-tail-on-the-donkey.
It was so dark.
Nobody needed blindfolds.

Then Mom told a spooky story.

It was about Iceman.

I had to admit it.

I was having fun.

The best part was when
Mom and Dad brought in
my big surprise.
It was a brand-new sled!

It had stopped snowing.

So we all went sledding.

The moon was full.

And snow, snow, snow

was everywhere.

Up and down the hill

we went.

When it got too cold,

we started back home.

We got to the front yard.

"Look!" said Dad.

He wrote "Happy Birthday"

in the snow.

"That's the

biggest card

you will ever get!"

"Lucky for me, it snowed!"
I said.
Then I heard my words.
Maybe I don't have such
bad luck after all.